WORD BIRD'S SHAPES

by Jane Belk Moncure
illustrated by Linda Hohag

THE CHILD'S WORLD

MANKATO, MN 56001

Library of Congress Cataloging in Publication Data

Moncure, Jane Belk.
  Word Bird's shapes.

  (Word Birds for early birds)
  Summary: Word Bird uses his blocks to build various shapes.
  [1. Birds—Fiction.   2. Size and shape—Fiction.
3. Vocabulary] I. Hohag, Linda, ill.   II. Title.
III. Series: Moncure, Jane Belk.   Word Birds for early birds.
PZ7.M739Wor   1983   [E]   83-15255
ISBN 0-89565-255-2 -1991 Edition

WORD BIRD'S SHAPES

Papa Bird gave
Word Bird a box
of squares—

red
squares
and...

blue
squares.

"I will make something
with my squares,"
Word Bird said.

Word Bird made
something square.

Mama Bird gave Word Bird a box of circles —

green
circles and...

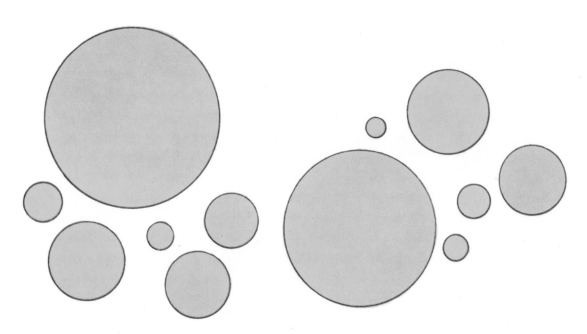

yellow circles.

"I will make something
with my circles,"
Word Bird said.

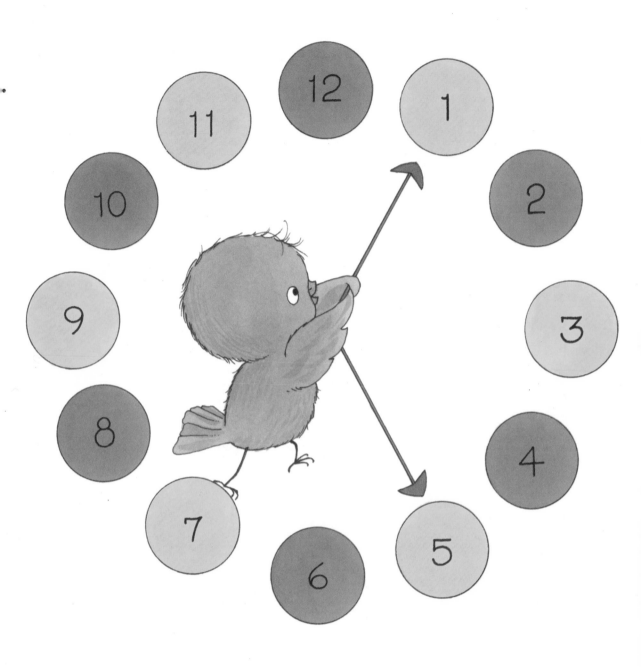

Word Bird made
something round.

Then Papa gave Word Bird a box of triangles—

orange
triangles and...

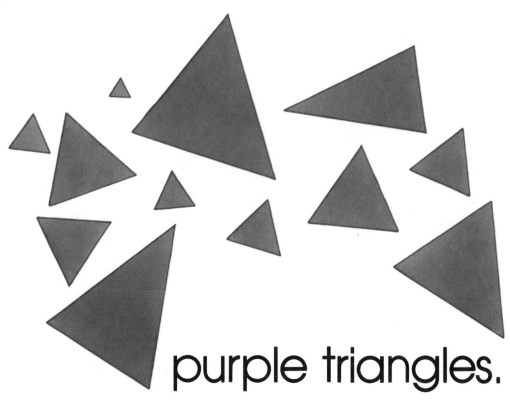

purple triangles.

"I will make something
with my triangles,"
Word Bird said.

Word Bird made a
big triangle.

Then Mama gave
Word Bird a box of
rectangles—

pink
rectangles
and...

brown
rectangles.

"I will make something
with my rectangles,"
Word Bird said.

Here is what
Word Bird made.

Then Mama said, "It is time to put your shapes away."

Word Bird put
the squares,
the circles,

the triangles,
the rectangles
in boxes.

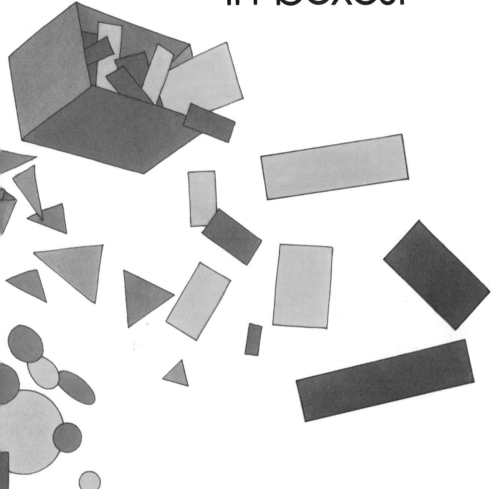

Then he TRIPPED.

Squares,

circles,

triangles,

and
rectangles

fell all over the floor.

"Look." said Papa.
"Look what you can
make now.

"With all the shapes,
you can make a
train.

"You can also make

a boat,

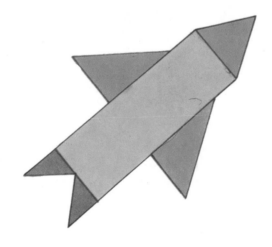

a plane,

a rocket,

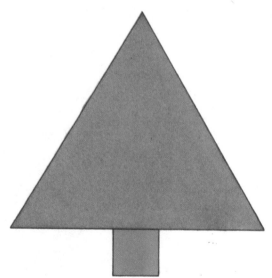

a tree...

a little
teepee,

a house,

a hat,

a truck,

and a cat.
What else?"

You can read these words with  **Word Bird.**

 square

 circle

 triangle

 rectangle

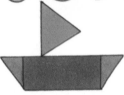 train

 boat

 plane

 rocket

 tree

 teepee

 house

 hat

 truck

cat

Now you make some shape pictures.